Team Building

David Stroud

TSL Drama

Characters

ANTONIO   Male nurse, about 35 years (Spanish)

DANNI   Nurse, about 25 years (from Yorkshire)

MICHAEL   Male nurse, about 30 years

PAUL   Unit manager, about 40 years

RACHEL   Psychoanalyst, about 50 years (Jewish)

STELLA   Assistant nurse, about 45 years

Setting

The sitting room of a beach apartment in Spain. Besides an opening to the outside (on the left side of the stage), three doors open from it: one to the bathroom, one to the men's bedroom, and one to the women's bedroom. On the right side is a kitchen area. Through a window is a view of the beach.

Performance time

40 minutes

Props

Seating for six people
Coffee table
Loose papers
Laptop
Mobile phone
Clipboard
Suitcases
Fridge
Large bowl, red liquid and glasses
Coffee mugs
Can of Coke
Small bottle of water
Packet for cakes

Sound Effects

Doorbell ringing
Toilet flushing

SCENE 1

Lights up.

ANTONIO is sitting by a coffee table, overflowing with papers, in front of a laptop, making notes. He picks up his mobile phone.

ANTONIO: Ah, Alfredo. Cómo estás? Is just to confirm the table for next Saturday night. Sí, at eight o'clock. Is the last day of our team building retreat and … team building? Is when people who work together go away and … oh, never mind. The last day of our holiday. Okay, but just make sure everything go smooth. These they are important people – very VIP, eh. No, of course they not speak Spanish. They are English. Yes, I know your policy – don't worry, we won't be late. Hasta luego.

ANTONIO hangs up, looks at his wristwatch, then carries on working.

Doorbell rings. ANTONIO goes to answer it.

ANTONIO: Hola, Paul.

PAUL enters with a suitcase.

PAUL: Hello, Antonio. Have the others arrived yet?

ANTONIO: No. You are the first. But I thought you would all be coming on the one plane.

PAUL: We did. But the five of us couldn't come in the same taxi.

ANTONIO: Ah, of course, no.

PAUL: And as the women wanted to look at the shops in the airport, I elected to take a taxi on my own. It was fifteen euros. Just make sure that comes off what I owe.

ANTONIO: Well, this is it, Paul. The apartment. This is the sitting room, and that is the kitchen-dining area over there. This is the first bedroom, and there is the second one. Better give this one to the women, I think. Is bigger, and you know what like they are. It has also the best view – of the beach.

PAUL: [*Imitating*] Yes, I know what like they are. But what's the other bedroom like?

ANTONIO *opens the door of the second bedroom and* PAUL *goes in. He comes out after a few seconds.*

PAUL: Yes, it's okay.

ANTONIO: [*picking up a clipboard from the coffee table*] Here is the timetable I make for the week. Of course, is fine if you want to change anything. Nothing is written on the stone. Tomorrow we get up at 0700 hours, have breakfast at 0730 hours. At 0830 hours we have our orientation meeting, followed at 0930 by –

PAUL: Hey, hold on, Antonio.

ANTONIO: What, you don't like? Is fine to change anything, is not written on the –

PAUL: I didn't say I don't like it. It's just that I think we should spend tomorrow chilling out. Getting to know each other a bit better. That's what this break is all about, after all.

ANTONIO: But I understood it was for team building.

PAUL: Yes, Antonio. But in our field team building is all about caring for each other. Understanding each others' needs. And the most important room?

ANTONIO *looks at him questioningly.*

PAUL: The toilet.

ANTONIO: Ah, yes. The bathroom, it is here.

PAUL *goes into the bathroom. With the door wide open, there is the sound of him urinating. The doorbell rings.* ANTONIO *carefully closes the bathroom door before going to open the main door. Enter* MICHAEL, STELLA, RACHEL *and* DANNI, *all carrying suitcases and talking at the same time.* ANTONIO *kisses the women and goes to kiss* MICHAEL, *who pulls back, putting out his hand instead.*

ANTONIO: Okay, girls, this is your bedroom.

All the women go into the bedroom.

DANNI: [*Off stage*] Fantastic!

STELLA: [*Off stage*] What a view!

RACHEL: [Off stage] Lovely writing desk!

ANTONIO: [*To* MICHAEL] And this is our bedroom.

MICHAEL: You mean yours, mine and Paul's?

ANTONIO: Of course, yes.

STELLA: [*As the three women come out*] Has the boss arrived yet?

Sound of the toilet flushing. PAUL *comes out.*

PAUL: Yes, he has.

ANTONIO: This is the bathroom.

MICHAEL: [*Aside*] I sort of guessed that.

DANNI, MICHAEL, RACHEL *and* STELLA *go into the bathroom.*

RACHEL: [*Coming out*] But where is the bath?

ANTONIO: There is not one, Rachel.

RACHEL: No bath?

ANTONIO: That is normal in Andalucía. Here, it is the custom to take showers only. I remember the old aunt of mine, she boasted of having a bath in her house. "But thank God we never had to use it," she used to say.

DANNI, MICHAEL, PAUL, RACHEL *and* STELLA *stare at him.*

ANTONIO: Because they bathed when they were ill only.

DANNI: Well, it's fine with me. I'd rather a shower any day. Especially a cold shower in this heat!

ANTONIO: Look what I make for you. [*He moves to the kitchen area and takes a large bowl out of the fridge*]

STELLA: Sangria!

ANTONIO: [*Ladling it into glasses*] But not like you buy it in Tesco's, no señor. Be careful, is quite strong.

PAUL: Is there anything different to drink?

ANTONIO: Is beer in the fridge.

In a semicircle they sit on the sofa, armchairs and wooden chairs drinking.

PAUL: On behalf of us all, I'd like to say thank you to Antonio for letting us stay in his apartment.

RACHEL: Yes, indeed. And for taking care of the financial arrangements.

DANNI, MICHAEL *and* STELLA *nod in agreement.*

ANTONIO: Oh, is nothing, really.

STELLA: [*Raising her glass*] And here's to Michael on his promotion to charge nurse.

DANNI: Congratulations!

ANTONIO: ¡Enhorabuena!

RACHEL, ANTONIO *and* DANNI *raise their glasses as well.* PAUL *does not.*

RACHEL: When do you take up your new position, Michael?

MICHAEL: As soon as we get back.

PAUL: [*Aside*] You wouldn't if I had my way.

RACHEL: And how does that make you feel?

DANNI: [*Giggling*] This is just like a sensitivity meeting at the Mental Health Unit.

STELLA: Oh, don't say that, Danni! I want to forget about the Unit for this week.

PAUL: I don't know why you work there if you despise what we do.

STELLA: [*Lifting a hand as if stopping traffic*] I'm not going to get involved in this type of conversation while I'm here. I've come here to have a break.

RACHEL: Would you like to talk about that, Stella?

STELLA: No … Why don't we all take a dip in the sea?

ANTONIO: Better wait till later, when the sun will have gone down a bit.

DANNI: [*Holding out her glass*] In that case, give me some more of this, Antonio. It's delish.

Lights down.

SCENE 2

Lights up.

Dawn. PAUL *is sitting by the window with a cup of coffee in his hand.* STELLA *enters from the women's bedroom in a bathrobe and goes into the bathroom without closing the door completely. Off stage: the sound of the shower and* STELLA *singing* Viva España *quietly in English.* PAUL *walks across the stage in a casual manner, trying to see through the bathroom door. He sits down on the opposite side, still staring at the bathroom door.*

STELLA *enters from the bathroom.*

STELLA: [*Startled*] I didn't see you there.

PAUL: You want a coffee?

STELLA: [*Hesitates, while drying her hair with a towel*] Yes, okay.

PAUL: [*Returning from the kitchen area with her coffee*] Did you guys have a good time last night?

STELLA: Yes. We went to that beach bar.

PAUL: Wish I could've come, but I had to get my report on Arthur finished.

STELLA: Poor thing.

PAUL: Well, I wanted to get it out of the way.

STELLA: No, I mean Arthur. One day he was participating in the therapy groups and next day … Have they held the inquest yet?

PAUL: No. It should be this week. But it's a foregone conclusion. He's had a dickey heart for years and he was no spring chicken. So the beach bar — or chiringuito, as Antonia calls it — was it good?

STELLA: His name is Antonio.

PAUL: Whatever.

STELLA: Yes, it was good. But afterwards …

PAUL: Afterwards …?

STELLA: Well, perhaps some of us had drunk a little bit too much.

PAUL: Who was there?

STELLA: All of us, except Rachel.

PAUL: She was writing up her dream diary.

STELLA: And you, of course.

PAUL: So what happened after the chiringuito?

STELLA: [*Stares at* PAUL *for a moment, then gets up*] I'm going to get dressed.

PAUL: Okay.

PAUL *watches her go into the women's bedroom, out of which comes DANNI.*

PAUL: Good morning, Danielle.

DANNI: You know I don't like being called that. Why do you have to call me that?

PAUL: Oh dear. What happened to you, then? Looks like you need a cup of coffee.

DANNI: Yes, I do. A strong one, please.

PAUL: [*Handing* DANNI *the coffee*] So what happened last night to make you all so sensitive?

DANNI: What makes you think something happened?

PAUL: No, it's just that, after you left the beach bar …

DANNI: Stella told you about it?

PAUL *nods and sips his coffee.*

DANNI: The sea looked so lovely.

PAUL: By the light of the silvery moon.

DANNI: We didn't have bathing costumes with us. "Who cares?" someone said. I think it was Michael.

PAUL: So you went skinny dipping?

DANNI: God, I've always hated that term. But, yes. It seemed like good fun at the time. I never knew sea water actually throws off sparks when you splash it at night. I imagined it would be completely dark.

PAUL: That's the plankton.

DANNI: I know. And when we came out of the water, we were, you know, because we had nothing to dry ourselves with, cuddling and laughing …

PAUL: In your skinny-dipping suits.

DANNI: The only thing that concerns me is ... well, it's my fiancé ... if he gets to hear about it. He wouldn't like it.

PAUL: Of course not. Not at his age.

DANNI: And I'm sure Stella's husband wouldn't like it either.

PAUL: No, not at his age.

DANNI: But they're completely different ages.

PAUL: You're right.

DANNI *looks confused.*

PAUL: One's too young and the other's too ... [*shrugs*] Perhaps we should establish a ground rule for the duration of our stay here.

DANNI: A ground rule?

PAUL: Yes. That is, whatever happens here will never be told to anyone who is not part of our present group. In that way, you won't have to worry about last night, and it will free us all up to do whatever we want. To just be ourselves.

DANNI: Sounds good to me. How did you think of that?

PAUL: I'm not the Unit manager for nothing.

DANNI: But will the others agree?

PAUL: Well, we can ask them. Let's have a meeting this morning, after breakfast.

DANNI: As far as I'm concerned, the sooner the better!

Lights down.

SCENE 3

Lights up.

ANTONIO, DANNI, MICHAEL, PAUL, RACHEL *and* STELLA *sitting in a semicircle.*

RACHEL: So, Paul, what you are suggesting is a rule of confidentiality?

PAUL: Yes. So everything that happens here, stays here, without exception. This would free us all up to really be ourselves, to express our personalities. I want this to be a neutral space.

RACHEL: [*Nodding*] After all, we're not here just on holiday, but to learn more about ourselves.

DANNI: And each other.

RACHEL: Yes, absolutely.

DANNI: Well, I'm all for it!

RACHEL: Has something happened that the rest of us should know about, then?

DANNI: Well, last night –

STELLA: Danni, we haven't established the rule yet.

DANNI: Right ...

PAUL: All those in favour of the rule, raise your hands.

            EVERYONE *raises their hand.*

PAUL: That's it, then. Motion carried, unanimously.

RACHEL: [*Hesitates*] I would like to propose something else. I know it might sound a bit odd, but … well, I'd like to keep a record of everyone's dreams while we are here. After all, it is a unique opportunity. Of course, it's only for those who want to participate. You see, it would be a history of our unconscious minds … just while we're here. We can analyse the results and – who knows? – maybe even publish them. What do you say?

PAUL: Sounds like a good idea to me. Stella?

STELLA: Yes, why not.

DANNI: Sounds great!

MICHAEL: Okay.

ANTONIO: I never remember my dreams.

RACHEL: That's probably because you don't normally pay attention to them.

ANTONIO: Okay, I am willing to give it a try.

            Silence.

STELLA: Is that it, then? Can we go now?

PAUL: Come on, you know we always allocate fifty minutes to our meetings.

DANNI: A psychoanalytic hour.

ANTONIO: [*Aside*]: With her being such a beautiful day outside!

            Silence.

RACHEL: I wonder what's going on here. Is it so difficult for us to look at ourselves in an environment away from the Unit?

Silence. STELLA, *dressed for the beach, with a large beach bag by her side, stares out of the window.*

Lights down.

SCENE 4

Lights up.

DANNI, MICHAEL, PAUL, RACHEL *and* STELLA *are finishing eating in the kitchen area.* ANTONIO *enters from the men's bedroom. His clothes, gait and mannerisms are effeminate.*

PAUL: Good God!

           DANNI *giggles.*

MICHAEL: [*Whispering*] Why is he dressed like that?

RACHEL: Well, didn't we agree that everyone could just be themselves with no come-back?

MICHAEL: But …

PAUL: You must have suspected he was like that.

ANTONIO: I am late, I am late!

PAUL: [*To the others*] That's all we need: Alice in Wonderland.

DANNI: Where are you going?

ANTONIO: To meet my friend of mine in the club in Torremolinos Centro.

PAUL: [*To the others*] It must be a gay club.

ANTONIO: Don't wait up for me, darlings.

MICHAEL: Wait, I'll come part of the way with you.

ANTONIO: Come then, chico, come, come. Roberto, his blood will burn if I am late. Adiós, guapos. [*Blows kisses to the others*] Mua mua.

ANTONIO *and* MICHAEL *exit.*

STELLA *and* DANNI *sit down on the sofa.*

RACHEL: Shall we carry on working on that dream you had last night, Paul?

PAUL *glances across at* STELLA *and* DANNI.

RACHEL: Come into our bedroom. You can lie on the bed. It'll be much more comfortable.

PAUL *and* RACHEL *exit into the women's bedroom.*

DANNI: I think it's super how Antonio has come out.

STELLA: Yes, it's an example to us all.

DANNI: I wish I could be as open as that.

STELLA: Why, is there something you would like to share with us?

DANNI: [*Hesitantly*] Maybe ... There was something in my early teens ... I've never told anyone about it. But now, here, with this rule of confidentiality ...

STELLA: You can tell me if you like. But wouldn't it be better to tell Rachel, or even Paul?

DANNI: I just think I'd feel more comfortable telling you.

STELLA: Well, I don't mind. What's it about?

DANNI: You know I was brought up on the Yorkshire Dales …
            There were no other kids living nearby, no one to play
            with.

STELLA: Yes. You must have been quite lonely.

DANNI: I was. Especially during the school holidays. So my
            parents got me a pet dog. A cross between an Alsatian
            and a retriever. He was the only friend I had during the
            long holidays. He was beautiful … [*She starts crying*]

STELLA: Are you sure you want to go on?

DANNI: Well … yes. As long as it doesn't upset you too much. I
            used to take him for long walks. We'd run through the
            grass, roll in the bracken. I loved him … no, I mean I
            really loved him. And I think he loved me.

STELLA: I can't see the problem, it's natural for –

DANNI: No, it wasn't natural. I began to have fantasies about
            him. Sexual fantasies. It wasn't natural!

            Taken aback, STELLA *covers her mouth with her hands.*

Lights down.

SCENE 5

Lights up.

A compact disk is playing flamenco music. ANTONIO *is dancing in an effeminate way, with a red carnation in his hair.* STELLA *is sitting in an armchair flipping through a magazine, glancing up at him with amusement now and again.*

ANTONIO: You don't know what a relief it has been for me to come out of the wardrobe!

STELLA: You mean closet.

ANTONIO: Cómo?

STELLA: It's been a relief for me to come out of the closet.

ANTONIO: What, you too?

STELLA: [*Laughing*] No, we say to come out of the closet, not the wardrobe.

ANTONIO: Ah, bueno.

STELLA: But you know something? I admire you for doing it.

ANTONIO: And I am grateful to Paul for him proposing that ground rule. It set me free. Free!

STELLA: What I don't understand is why you went to live in London when you were living in such a beautiful place as this.

ANTONIO: Well, the truth is, Estelita, there is a skeleton in my wardrobe.

STELLA: Cupboard.

ANTONIO: Cómo?

STELLA: There's a skeleton in my cupboard.

ANTONIO: In yours too, eh?

STELLA: You really do have problems with your wardrobes and cupboards, don't you?

ANTONIO: [*Sitting down and facing* STELLA] Anyway, what happened was that …

PAUL enters from the main door, wearing a long-sleeved shirt, long trousers, a wide-brimmed hat and sun glasses.

STELLA: [*Sarcastically*] You've been taking the sun?

PAUL: I've just been for a walk along the promenade.

PAUL takes a beer from the fridge.

ANTONIO: [*Whispering to* STELLA] The skeleton, I will tell you about him another time.

ANTONIO goes into the men's bedroom.

PAUL sits near STELLA and sips his beer.

STELLA: I am so happy that you suggested that ground rule.

PAUL: At last I've done something right in your eyes.

STELLA: Oh, I've never said you were all bad … It's wonderful how you've allowed Antonio to come out of the closet – or wardrobe, as he puts it. And Danni has been very open with me. Told me about what happened to her as a child.

PAUL: What happened to her?

STELLA: [*Hesitates*] It's confidential. Anyway, I don't want to talk about it. It really upset me.

PAUL: It's the things that upset us that can teach us most.

STELLA: Yes, yes. But no, no I don't want to talk about it. Even Antonio was going to tell me his dark secret when you walked in.

PAUL: So can we expect you to come out of your shell soon?

STELLA: [*Surprised*] I really don't have anything to ...

PAUL: Oh, I don't know. Being married to someone sixteen years older than you, doesn't that cause problems?

STELLA: Age isn't the most important thing in a relationship.

PAUL: I wouldn't know.

STELLA: Well, Paul, wouldn't you say it's a little unusual for someone of your age to still be single? Now, don't try to tell me that being single doesn't bring its own problems.

PAUL: So how did it come about that you married an older man?

STELLA: I was a young staff nurse when I met him. He was a distinguished, mature doctor. But very young to be a consultant.

PAUL: You must have been very pretty.

STELLA: Must have been?

PAUL: [*Disconcerted*] What I meant was … you still are, but …

STELLA: It's too late now. You've said it … Anyway, when our little girl grew up I wanted to go back to work. The Mental Health Unit was close by. It was easy for Percy to get me a job there … you know, being one of the consultants.

PAUL: That was two years ago. In fact, I remember your first day. There was something about you.

STELLA: Now I'm not sure that it was a good idea. Coming to work in the Unit, I mean. I've mentioned to him that perhaps I should look for a post somewhere else. Before coming to work at the Unit I had no idea of the way most of the staff saw him … As someone who didn't fit in.

PAUL: The description I've heard is, "As dull as dishwater".

STELLA: Hey!

PAUL: Anything goes, remember?

STELLA: [*Relaxing again*] Yes, you're right.

PAUL: The fact is, Stella, that is how we see him at the Unit.

STELLA: He's a practical, down to earth man, that's all.

PAUL: Sure, but he's a man who doesn't understand psycho-dynamic theory. For him, it seems the unconscious doesn't exist.

STELLA: Is that why you despise him?

PAUL: Well, it's not easy for us to work with a consultant psychiatrist like that.

MICHAEL enters from the men's bedroom, in shorts and a tee-shirt.

MICHAEL: Just going for a run before lunch. Ciao. [*Exits by the main door*]

PAUL: Ciao? He doesn't even know what country he's in. What do you think about him?

STELLA: Who?

PAUL: Him. Our very own Adonis.

STELLA: Oh, he's not a bad kid.

PAUL: He doesn't think about anything except keeping fit.

STELLA: [*Smiling coyly*] Oh, I wouldn't say that.

PAUL: Sounds like you know something I don't.

STELLA: Well, I know ... I know he thinks about certain other things.

PAUL: Come on, Stella, out with it. What else does he think about, in your opinion?

STELLA: He thinks about, well ... sex, for instance.

PAUL: And how would you know that?

STELLA: No, no – I really shouldn't say anything.

PAUL: I see. So it's okay for others to expose their inner

selves – like Antonia and Danni – but not for you. Is that it?

STELLA: [*Thinks for a moment*] You're right. It's hypocritical, isn't it? Okay, I'm going to tell you what happened. It was when we were on night duty together last year … no, no, I shouldn't tell you.

PAUL: Go on, Stella, why not break a habit of a lifetime? You can always stop, at any time, if it's too much for you.

STELLA: That's true. Well, it was during those few weeks, when we were on nights together …

PAUL: You already said that.

STELLA: … that he … propositioned me.

PAUL: Propositioned you?

STELLA: Yes, you know. Asked me to … you know. "Come on," he said, "there's an empty bed in one of the side rooms we can use. Nobody will ever know." At first I thought he was joking. But then I realised he meant business.

PAUL: So what did you do?

STELLA: What do you think? That I jumped into bed with him? No, I told him to sod off.

PAUL: And did he carry on harassing you?

STELLA: Well, it wasn't harassment, really.

PAUL: No, because I bet deep down one hot little Stella was lapping it up.

STELLA: How dare you! What do you take me for?

            PAUL *shrugs his shoulders.*

STELLA: [*Getting up*] It just wasn't like that.

PAUL: Then why did you get so angry when I said it?

STELLA: Oh, I've had enough of this crap! I'm going to bed. Good night!

            STELLA *exits into the women's bedroom, slamming the door after her.*

Lights down.

SCENE 6

Lights up.

ANTONIO, PAUL, MICHAEL, RACHEL *and* STELLA.

RACHEL: Morning, everyone. Now let's see. Who had a dream last night? Anyone? ... Anything? Come on, someone must remember something, even if it's just a fragment.

STELLA: Me, I was afraid to dream. There was a total blackout.

MICHAEL: [*Doing press-ups*] I had a dream about going to change something at Marks and Sparks, but it didn't make sense. The strange thing is, though, it left me feeling disturbed.

RACHEL: Dreams always make sense, Michael. It's just a matter of finding out what they mean.

MICHAEL: Besides, I don't really see the point in analysing them.

RACHEL: According to Freud, dreams are the royal road to the unconscious. Come and lie down here [*indicates the sofa*] and we'll try to see what it means.

MICHAEL: Okay, but after my run.

   MICHAEL *hangs a hand towel around his neck and leaves by the main door.*

RACHEL: [*Follows him with her eyes*] Oh, vey, as if he hasn't done enough exercise already.

PAUL: All brawn no brains, that's Mikey.

RACHEL *looks at him sharply.*

PAUL: And he thinks he's God's gift to women.

RACHEL: In other words, everything you are not.

PAUL: I think that's bang out of order, Rachel. For once, you're way off the mark. I mean, I don't mind doing a few press-ups or even a bit of jogging now and again, but not to be fanatical like him.

RACHEL: Is that why you try to control him so much in the Unit?

PAUL: Come on, Rachel, it's not a matter of trying to control him. Perhaps it's true I don't really have much faith in him, but ... well, some people need more supervision than others. Let's face it, he's got the sensitivity of a cockroach.

RACHEL: And you believe that by controlling him you can also control your own anxiety? Isn't that the truth, too?

STELLA: This apartment is turning out to be like the Unit, with psychodynamics flying around all over the place.

PAUL: Don't be so cynical, Stella. You sound like that damn husband of yours!

RACHEL: Our stay here isn't just a holiday. It's an opportunity to learn more about ourselves as a team.

PAUL: A team building exercise.

RACHEL: For that we need a model, and the one we are accustomed to is the psychodynamic model.

STELLA: What I don't understand is, why it's called 'dynamic' when the only thing you do is sit around talking.

RACHEL: [*Smiling patiently*] It's called dynamic because it deals with the flow of energy from one part of the psyche to another – that is, between the conscious, the unconscious, the ego and the super-ego. You see?

ANTONIO: [*Whispering*] She has the Jewish disease bad, bad.

STELLA: [*Whispering*] What disease is that?

ANTONIO: [*Whispering*] Psychoanalysis.

Lights down.

SCENE 7

Lights up.

The early hours of the morning. STELLA enters from the women's bedroom in a bathrobe. She takes a can of Coke from the fridge, pours it into a glass and drinks. MICHAEL enters from the men's bedroom, wearing only his underpants.

MICHAEL: [*Surprised to see* STELLA] What's up? Can't you sleep?

STELLA: No. It's so hot. And you?

MICHAEL: I just got up for some water. [*Takes a small bottle of water from the fridge*]

STELLA: You know, when I heard the door opening, I hoped it was you.

MICHAEL: Why?

STELLA: Because … it's been so long since we've had the chance to talk alone.

MICHAEL *looks at her.*

STELLA: Tell me, do you still think about … what we talked about when we were on nights together?

MICHAEL: Yes, but as you said then, you weren't interested …

STELLA: And are you still curious …

MICHAEL: Curious …?

STELLA: Yes, I mean, about … the position … my favourite …

MICHAEL: I'm sorry. I shouldn't have asked you that.

STELLA: [*Touching his face*] You're so beautiful … Do you want me to tell you? Or show you?

MICHAEL: Are you playing games with me?

STELLA: Yes, I suppose I am. But that's all right here, isn't it? I mean, this is supposed to be a neutral space. More than that, it's magical.

STELLA kisses his chest and goes downward until she is kneeling in front of him. When she stands up again he draws her towards him.

STELLA: Wait. Have you got something to put on?

MICHAEL: To put on? Oh, yes. I'll get it.

MICHAEL exits into the men's bedroom and STELLA goes to sit on the sofa. He enters and, sitting next to her on the sofa, embraces and kisses her.

STELLA draws away and looks at him questioningly.

MICHAEL: It's okay. I've put it on.

STELLA relaxes into his arms again.

MICHAEL: I've missed you so much.

STELLA: [*Putting her finger to his mouth to silence him*] You don't have to say things like that.

They carry on kissing and fondling each other.

STELLA: Michael …

MICHAEL: Yes, Stella?

STELLA: Switch the light off.

MICHAEL gets up and switches the light off.

The stage is now in total darkness. After about 30 seconds, moans and gasps can be heard.

After a while, the door of the men's bedroom opens and PAUL enters, faintly lit by the light from the bedroom.

MICHAEL: [*Whispering*] Oh, Stella, Stella ...

PAUL exits back into the bedroom, closing the door sharply behind him.

MICHAEL: Who was that?

STELLA: Oh, my God!

Lights down.

SCENE 8

Lights up.

PAUL enters. Goes to the kitchen area. Takes a packet and moves towards STELLA, who is sitting on the sofa.

PAUL: Antonia bought these in Torremolinos for us.

STELLA: It's Antonio.

PAUL: Whatever. He said we should have them with drinking chocolate. But I suppose coffee will do.

           STELLA takes what looks like an elongated doughnut.

STELLA: Hmm. Delicious! What are they?

PAUL: Churros. The Spanish version of a doughnut.

           They eat and drink their coffee.

PAUL: Listen, Stella, I've got to tell you something.

STELLA: Yes?

PAUL: It's got to do with what you told me yesterday.

           STELLA stops chewing.

STELLA: What, specifically?

PAUL: About Mikey's sexual harassment.

STELLA: It wasn't sexual harassment!

PAUL: Perhaps you didn't see it like that –

STELLA: Because it wasn't like that!

PAUL: You have to understand that sexual harassment affects other people who are around, not only the one being harassed.

STELLA: Who are you talking about?

PAUL: The patients.

STELLA: It didn't affect them at all! They didn't know anything about it.

PAUL: Consciously, maybe not. But unconsciously ...

STELLA: What the shit are you talking about?

PAUL: Pardon?

STELLA: I've had psychobabble up to here [*Indicates the top of her head*]

PAUL: Be that as it may, I've decided that I must act on the information I have concerning you and Mikey.

STELLA: What do you mean?

PAUL: I've thought it over very carefully. It wasn't an easy decision ...

STELLA: What decision?

PAUL: To discipline Mikey. I'll inform Percy as soon as we get back.

STELLA: My husband ... you're going to tell my husband?

PAUL: He has to be involved in any disciplinary action. Besides, he was on the panel which selected Mikey for promotion. They might want to reconsider their decision.

STELLA: So it was you last night, who came out ...?

PAUL: I'm not talking about last night. I'm talking about when you were on night duty, the sexual harassment.

STELLA: Who are you trying to fool? This is about what happened last night.

PAUL: What happened last night? Tell me more, do.

STELLA: You can't, Paul ... you can't ... What about the rule – that everything here is confidential?

PAUL: But that didn't happen here. That happened in the Unit. While you were both on duty. Do you want another one of these? [*He offers her the packet of churros*] No? Okay, I'll put them back.

         PAUL *returns the packet to the kitchen area, then puts on his straw hat.*

PAUL: A nice stroll along the promenade before lunch, I think. See you later.

         PAUL *leaves by the main door, leaving STELLA staring after him, stunned.*

Lights fade and go out.